DRAKE'S D[

C000093341

A Tudo

By Pauline Francis

Illustrated by Gillian Marklew

ANGLIA *young* BOOKS

First published in 1998
by Anglia Young Books
Durhams Farmhouse
Ickleton
Saffron Walden, Essex CB10 1SR

Illustrations by Gillian Marklew

British Library Cataloguing-in-Publication Data

A catalogue record for this book is available from the
British Library

ISBN 1 871173 56 6

Typeset in Palatino by Goodfellow & Egan, Cambridge
and printed in Great Britain by Ashford Colour Press,
Gosport, Hampshire

For Daniel and Anna

DRAKE'S VOYAGE AROUND THE WORLD
1577–1580 (see map)

December, 1577:	Drake leaves Plymouth, England. Crosses the Atlantic Ocean and the Equator. Sails along the coast of Brazil
June, 1578:	Port St. Julian
November, 1578:	Island of Mocha, off the coast of Chile
March, 1579:	Off the coasts of Ecuador and Mexico
July, 1579:	California
October, 1579:	The Philippine Islands
March, 1580:	Java
July, 1580:	Sierra Leone, West Africa
September, 1580:	Plymouth, England

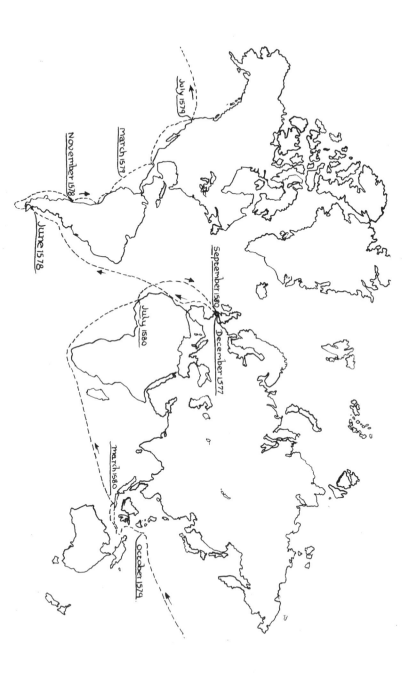

CHAPTER ONE

It was a raw December day in 1577. Will Thatcher shivered on the quayside of Plymouth Hoe as he waited for his father. He didn't recognise the ships in the harbour so perhaps it was true that Francis Drake had returned to Plymouth.

A ship named the *Pelican* lay in the water close enough for Will to count seven gun holes on each side. Men swarmed over the masts and rigging like monkeys, whistling and shouting to each other. The rest of the harbour was alive with small wooden boats, ferrying baskets and barrels out to the ships.

Will's father rowed his boat alongside the harbour wall.

'Over here, lad!' he shouted.

Will ran to join him and they stood for a moment looking out at the *Pelican*.

'Is it true that Francis Drake is the captain of the *Pelican*?' asked Will.

'It is,' said his father. 'What I would give to sail in a ship like that. And he's a generous captain. I've loaded tons of salt herring and barrels of beer. Mind you, they say he's taking on ninety men.'

He looked wearily at Will.

'You do the afternoon runs, Will,' he said. 'I've business to do before dark. Take any job you are offered. There's eight of us to feed now.'

Will watched his father disappear between the rickety timbered houses overlooking the harbour. The sun came out and Will dangled his legs over the edge of the quay, watching the ships rock backwards and forwards in the winter wind.

'Where *is* my boat?' came an irritable voice behind him. 'I told Moone to fetch me by two o' the clock.'

'Patience, master,' someone replied. 'He'll be along soon.'

Will turned to see who was speaking. The young, dark skinned man was simply dressed but the older one wore red velvet breeches and a jacket, each trimmed with gold braid. He tugged at his pointed beard and the tassel on his hat swung as he looked round impatiently.

'I'll wait no longer!' he said. 'Find me a boat, Diego. Now!'

Will sprang to his feet in front of the men.

'William Thatcher, gentlemen,' he said with a slight bow. 'At your service.'

The bearded man looked down at Will.

'Are you strong enough for the job, Will Thatcher?' he asked.

'Yes, Sir,' said Will, 'I am.'

'Then row us out,' he said.

The boat sank low in the water as the two men climbed in. Will pulled hard on the oars and soon they were clear of the quayside.

'Which ship is it, Sir?' he asked.

But, instead of answering Will direct, the man said:

'Tell me, boy, do you know who I am?'

'No, Sir,' said Will.

The man slapped his thigh and roared with laughter.

'If I tell you to take me to that fine ship over there, the one called the *Pelican*, would you know me then?'

Will stopped rowing when he realised who his passenger was and the boat bobbed up and down on the water.

'You're Francis Drake!' he said at last, pulling on the oars again.

'The very same,' said Drake. 'And this is my manservant, Diego. What have you heard about me, William Thatcher?'

Will looked embarrassed.

'That you rob Spanish ships and bring back treasure for Queen Elizabeth,' he muttered. 'And that it has made you a rich man.'

'Then you've heard right!' laughed Drake. 'I've sailed to the Spanish Main three times in as many years.'

'Where's that?' asked Will.

Francis Drake looked past the *Pelican* and beyond the harbour walls to the horizon.

'If you sail past the coast of Spain,' he said softly, 'you enter an ocean with waves taller than my ship, and fish that leap out of the water. And if you cross that ocean, you come to islands where the sun beats down every day, and brightly coloured birds. . ..'

'Are there monkeys?' Will asked, excited.

'Of the brightest silver,' said Drake.

'And Spanish ships full of gold!' laughed Diego.

They went the rest of the way in silence until they came alongside the *Pelican*.

'What do you think of my ship, Will Thatcher?' asked Drake. 'Seventy feet from stem to stern though she leaks a bit when the seas are high.'

Will gazed up at the gleaming timbers of the *Pelican* until he felt dizzy. He turned to Francis Drake.

'It's the finest sight I have ever seen,' he said.

Francis Drake stared at Will.

'How old are you, Will?' he asked.

'Nearly thirteen.'

'The same age as me when I first went to sea,' said Francis Drake. 'I've a mind to take you with me, boy. What do you think? Will you sail with me to the coast of North Africa to bring back fruits for our Queen?'

Will stared at Francis Drake, remembering his father's words. 'Take any job you are offered, there are eight of us to feed now.' And he might see silver monkeys.

Had he the courage to go?

Will stood up in the boat and, hardly recognising his own voice, shouted

'Yes, Sir, I'll come with you!'

***

Will sailed the next morning, just before dawn when the tide was high. His father rowed him across to the *Pelican* which was still lit with lanterns. Will said goodbye and turned quickly to climb the rope ladder, his eyes stinging with salt spray and tears. A boy with fair curly hair was waiting at the top.

'Welcome aboard!' he said. 'I'm Brewer.'

'Will Thatcher,' said Will shyly.

'I'm the trumpeter,' said Brewer. 'Do you know what you'll be doing?'

'No,' said Will. 'I've never been to sea before.'

Will had no time to look around him. He was taken immediately below deck. The stench of fish and salt made him feel sick and he wiped his foreheard. Brewer turned to look at him.

'You'll get used to the smell,' he said. 'And wait until you see where we have to sleep. We're right next to the cooking gallery and when the fire's lit, you can hardly breathe. But we sleep on deck as soon as the weather gets warmer.'

They went deeper into the ship, past the gun deck, until they were below the water-line where the only light came from flickering candles.

Brewer stopped and pointed to a plank of wood between the creaking timbers.

'You can sleep here, next to me, if you like. The ship's carpenter sleeps here, too. You'll like him. He's called Moone and I've sailed with him before.'

Brewer looked at Will's small bundles of clothes.

'Have you got a box?' he asked.

Will shook his head.

Brewer looked at Will's worried face and pulled out a small wooden box from under his plank. He hesitated for a moment, then gave it to Will.

'You can use this one,' he said quietly. 'It belonged to my friend. He was killed during an attack on the Spanish main.'

Will didn't know what to say. He opened the box. Inside was a wooden plate, a cup, a knife, a piece of string, half a candle and a few nails.'

'Thank you,' he said at last. 'I'll look after it well.'

'Only three rules on this ship,' said Brewer. 'No gambling, no throwing dice and no swearing. Captain Drake is a fair man but he'll punish anybody who breaks his rules.'

As Will listened to Brewer, he sweated more and more in the stifling atmosphere of the ship. He wanted to run up to the deck and call his father to take him back home. He bit his lip hard. If he wanted to see all the wonders over the horizon, he would have to be braver than this. Then Will heard the clank of metal below his feet and he felt the ship rock from side to side.

'Anchor's away,' said Brewer. 'Let's get on deck.'

Men were rushing across the deck to get the *Pelican* under way. Will was nearly knocked off his feet by a man who shouted at him, 'Out of my way, boy, there's work to do!' Brewer pulled Will towards the ship's rail where they watched the quay become smaller and smaller as the *Pelican* gathered speed.

Soon they were through the harbour entrance and the sails flapped in the wind. The *Pelican* dipped and rose through the Channel, followed closely by the other ships in the expedition.

'The one just behind us is the *Elizabeth*,' shouted Brewer. 'Then the *Marigold* and the *Swan*. The last one, that little one, is the *Christopher*.'

Will was surprised to see a group of men in velvet costumes and feathered hats walking the deck.

'Who are they?' he asked.

'Our gentlemen-travellers,' said Brewer, pulling a face. 'They've come for adventure and paid well to do it. The one with the book in his hand is Captain Thomas Doughty, a good friend of Captain Drake, they say. I don't know who the others are.'

Will clutched the rail and watched the waves become wider and taller and frothy with foam. The wind howled through the rigging and heavy rain began to beat the canvas like a drum. Will longed for the ship to stop moving so that he could be still. He began to shiver and moan and clutch his stomach.

'Brewer,' he gasped. 'I need the privy.'

'You're right next to it.'

'Where?' groaned Will.

'See that plank over the water, the one with holes in it?' said Brewer.

'I only want to be sick,' said Will, unable to stop his teeth chattering.

'Then you're best where you are,' said Brewer. 'I've got to report to the captain, then I'll come back up for you.'

Now Will was alone on the deck apart from Thomas Doughty who closed his book and came over to Will.

'Here, boy,' he said coldly. 'Take this to my cabin. I shall stay and walk the deck.'

Will felt his stomach lurch as the ship rose into the air.

'Take it, boy!'

Will leaned forward to take the book, but as he did so, he was violently sick over the silver buckles of Thomas Doughty's shoes. Doughty stepped back quickly and raised his arm as if to strike Will with the book; but instead, he turned away, shouting angrily over his shoulder

'Be careful in the future, boy. I shall be watching you.'

Will lay groaning on the deck. Already he had made an enemy. At that moment, he wished with all his heart that he was still safely tucked up in bed at home.

CHAPTER TWO

Will was sick for days. He told himself that if ever he got back to Plymouth, he would never leave land again, not even to help his father on the boat.

But at last he began to feel better and even found the movement of the ship soothing. Soon he was well enough to get up.

'I've been sick all over my clothes,' Will told Moone. 'They stink.'

'You don't need to tell me that, lad,' laughed Moone. 'You'll be given fresh clothes, but they'll have to do you the whole voyage.'

Brewer fetched them for Will. Canvas breeches, a leather jerkin, a woollen cap and a rough linen shirt which made Will's skin itch.

'Don't worry about the itching,' said Brewer. 'You'll soon be full of fleas like the rest of us.' He paused. 'Captain Drake wants to see you.'

Will's heart thumped.

'Am I in trouble for not working?' he asked.

Brewer laughed.

'No! I've told you before, the captain's a fair man,' he said. 'He remembers his first time at sea. We all do. It's something you never forget. I'd better take you to his cabin. It's at the other end of the ship.'

Will's eyes opened wide when Diego showed him into Captain Drake's cabin. Its walls were of gleaming wood and an enormous carved bed took up most of the space. At its side was a writing table and a large oak chest. Francis Drake put down his quill, blotted the book in which he was writing and closed it.

'So, Master Will, they tell me you've been sick.'

'Yes, Sir,' said Will. 'But I'm ready to work now. I can cook, wait at table, scrub the deck. I could climb the mast.'

'I've something else in mind for you, boy,' said Drake. 'You see the oak chest there? Open it.'

Will lifted the heavy lid. Its underneath was decorated with ships in full sail.

'The ship in the middle is the *Pelican*,' said Drake. 'Now lift out the bundle you see inside. Be careful. Then take off the blanket.'

Will did as he was told and brought out a wooden drum edged with red. He touched the coat of arms painted on it, then the ship and globe above. He leaned forward, trying to read the strange words written below.

Drake watched him.

'*Sic magna parvis*,' he said. 'Latin. It means "Great

things from small beginnings". My family motto, Will. What do you think of my drum? It cost me dear.'

'It's beautiful,' said Will. 'Who will beat it?'

'You,' said Drake. 'I think you will make a fine drummer boy. You are tall and thin and your arms are long. Brewer will teach you. I had him in mind to beat my drum but he declares he is only a trumpeter. The boy is right. He is too short for the side drum.'

'But how will I have the time?' asked Will, puzzled. 'We'll be back in Plymouth long before I have learned.'

Francis Drake came over and touched the globe on the drum.

'There will be plenty of time, Will, you can be sure of that,' he said quietly. 'Now go and tell Brewer the good news for he never wanted to be a drummer boy. Take the drum with you.'

Will rushed out of the cabin and up the dark stairs. At the top he ran into someone standing in the shadows.

'Watch where you're going, boy,' said a stern voice.

Will was pulled roughly onto the deck where, in the dazzling sunlight, he looked up into the furious face of Thomas Doughty. The man grabbed hold of Will by the collar and lifted him from the deck until Will was level with Doughty's cold eyes. Then Doughty pulled Will so close that he felt the man's beard scratch his cheeks.

'Do you remember me, boy?'

'Yes,' whispered Will. 'You're Master Doughty.'

'Captain Doughty, and friend of Captain Drake, don't forget.'

Doughty looked at the drum.

'So you're to be Drake's drummer boy?'

'Yes, Sir,' said Will.

'How will you have time to learn?' asked Doughty. 'We are nearly at the coast of Africa.'

'I don't know, Sir,' said Will.

Doughty shook Will until his head began to spin and he felt sick.

'Tell me what the captain said!' said Doughty.

'He just touched the globe on the drum and said I would have plenty of time,' said Will, trembling. 'I don't know what he meant.'

Doughty put him back down on the deck with such force that Will's teeth rattled.

'Thank you, drummer boy. That's all I wanted to know.'

Will ran to find Brewer.

'I'm going to be Captain Drake's drummer boy!' he said, holding up the drum.

Brewer slapped him on the back.

'Good for you, Will,' he said. 'And for me! Can you imagine me playing a drum, even such a fine one as this!'

'No!' laughed Will. His face became serious as he remembered the incident with Doughty.

'I met Captain Doughty. He kept asking me strange questions,' said Will.

'I've heard rumours,' said Brewer. 'They say there's trouble brewing between Doughty and Captain Drake.'

'What sort of trouble?' asked Will.

'Doughty has heard that Drake plans to cross the ocean.'

Will's eyes opened wide.

'To the Spanish Main?' he asked.

'No,' said Brewer. 'Further south than that.'

'But I thought we were sailing to North Africa and back,' said Will.

Brewer nodded.

'That's what Captain Drake told us. There's going to be trouble all right. I'm not too pleased myself, if it is true; but I expect the Queen knows about it. She and Drake understand one another very well. But Captain Drake will have to speak out soon.'

Brewer was right. Francis Drake announced his plans the very next day. He addressed the full ship's company and showed them a rolled up parchment tied with ribbon.

'I have orders here from her Majesty, Queen

Elizabeth, to make contact with the rulers of *Terra Australis*.'

'So you mean to take us all to the ends of the earth,' shouted Doughty. 'By God, Drake, you have deceived us all. And pray how will we get there?'

'Through the Strait of Magellan,' said Drake.

Brewer gasped. Will turned to him.

'What's wrong?' he whispered.

'No Englishman has ever sailed through the Strait of Magellan and come out alive,' said Brewer. 'It is the most dangerous water on earth.'

Doughty was speaking again.

'And what if we refuse?' he asked.

Drake looked him full in the face.

'You know the punishment for treason,' he said quietly.

Doughty turned angrily and left the deck. Drake watched him then spoke again to his crew.

'You have nothing to fear,' he said. 'I shall look after you well.'

The men drifted away, muttering among themselves.

'No wonder the captain said you'd have plenty of time to learn the drum!' said Brewer.

'You'll have plenty of time all right, lads,' said Moone. 'Never mind the Strait. We might never get as far as that.'

'Why not?' asked Will.

Moone looked worried.

'I've heard terrible things about that part of the ocean,' he said. 'It's called the Doldrums. Not a breath of wind to fill the sails for weeks. Drinking water all green and slimy in the stifling heat, and rotting food, and. . ..'

Brewer shook his head at Moone.

'We'll just have to trust to God,' he said.

They sailed into the Doldrums four weeks later. The *Pelican* drifted for fifteen days. Men began to fall ill and some died of fever. Moone sat on the deck carving a new set of buttons for his jacket from cheese that was too hard to eat. Even the captain was anxious.

Will wanted to do more than drum the men to deck and he began to feel restless. To calm himself, he sat in the shade of the sail and beat the drum softly, hour after hour. It was the only sound to break the eerie silence of the calm ocean. Thomas Doughty found him and shouted angrily, 'Stop that noise!'

Will shivered and put down the drum sticks. He had the feeling that something terrible was going to happen soon.

CHAPTER THREE

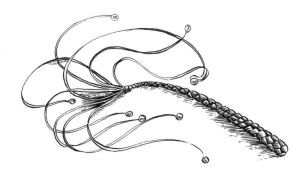

Trouble started as soon as they left the Doldrums. The sails suddenly took in wind and the *Pelican* captured a Portuguese ship. This new ship joined Drake's fleet under an English name, the *Mary*.

Brewer came to find Will on deck.

'I've come to say goodbye, Will,' he said.

'Where are you going?' asked Will, anxious.

'Captain Doughty has been sent to command the *Mary*,' said Brewer. 'Don't ask me why. He's not a sea-captain. I think Captain Drake is sick of him stirring up trouble. This way, he'll be rid of Doughty. I'm to keep an eye on him.'

'I wish I could come with you,' said Will, watching Brewer climb down the ladder.

'Just make sure you beat that drum bravely,' Brewer shouted back. 'After all, I've taught you well!'

A few days later, Will was on deck watching Captain Drake sketch the coast of Brazil, when a small boat came alongside the *Pelican*. Brewer scrambled aboard and went straight up to Drake, so angry that he didn't notice Will.

'What is it, Brewer?' asked Drake, putting down his quill pen and ink.

'Sir, I am sent to tell you that Thomas Doughty is stealing the Portuguese treasure from the hold of the ship and taking it to his cabin.'

'I ordered it to be kept under lock,' Francis Drake shouted. 'I will not have this! Doughty will be brought back here! I shall give him one more chance. He shall command this ship where the other gentlemen travellers will keep him in order.'

'Who will command the *Mary*, Sir?' asked Brewer.

'I shall go aboard myself,' said the captain.

The changeover took place straight away. Will didn't like the atmosphere on board the *Pelican*. When he drummed the men to deck, they came slowly, grumbling and whispering.

'Can't you do a better job than that, Drake's drummer boy?' asked Doughty and made the men laugh.

They sailed down the coast of Brazil. There were strange fogs and sudden high winds which rained sand on the ship's deck. The crew became nervous and Doughty took pleasure in making them feel worse.

'The natives along this coast have kept their freedom,' he told them, 'because of their magic powers. That's why the Spanish haven't settled there. You see those fires on the hills?'

The men nodded.

'They're making sacrifices to the devil. They can call up the devil in any shape. A lion, a tiger. . ..' Doughty stared at them . . .. 'even the shape of a man who will take you through dangerous water to your deaths.'

The men glanced at one another, frightened.

One day, when Will thought he could not stand the bad atmosphere any longer, he was relieved to see Brewer come aboard again.

'What do you want?' Doughty asked Brewer coldly.

'Captain Drake has sent me to ask how things are aboard the *Pelican*, Sir,' said Brewer.

'Has he now!' said Doughty slowly. 'Well, we'll show you how we treat spies on this ship!'

Doughty nodded to the men.

'Give him the cobbey!' he shouted.

The men circled round Brewer as he turned and tried to scramble back down the ladder. One of the men caught the back of his breeches and pulled them down. Another picked up a cat o' nine tails and began to whip Brewer.

Will watched in horror.

'Stop!' he shouted. 'Stop it!'

'Be quiet, drummer boy,' said Doughty, 'or you'll be next.'

Will flinched as the men took it in turn to lash Brewer.

'Stay out of it, Will,' his friend gasped. 'There's nothing you can do.'

'Yes, there is,' thought Will and he crept quietly down to the store room, afraid that someone would follow him. He took the drum and made for the upper deck facing the *Mary*.

Doughty saw him.

'Bring the drummer boy down here to me!' he shouted to the men.

It was now or never. Will stood tall and raised the drumsticks high into the air as Brewer had taught him, and beat the drum. The sound vibrated through the waves and reached the ears of Francis Drake who rushed over to the rail of the *Mary*.

'By God, it's young Will beating my drum!' he shouted. 'There must be danger! Prepare to board the *Pelican*!'

Will carried on drumming until he was dragged down to the lower deck where Moone was helping Brewer to his feet.

Doughty snatched the drum from Will.

'I warned you, drummer boy,' he said.

'The boy didn't mean any harm, Sir,' shouted Moone.

There were murmurs of support for Moone. Doughty pushed the carpenter away from Brewer's side.

'Keep quiet!' he said.

Then he turned to Will.

'Thanks to you, Drake is coming aboard.'

He shouted to the men

'Take the drummer boy and his spying friend below. I shall deal with Captain Drake.'

As Doughty spoke, he touched his sword lightly and moved towards the ship's rail. Silence fell over the deck.

Will and Brewer were thrown into a store room where Brewer lay on the floor, groaning with pain.

'What if Doughty takes Drake prisoner as well?' gasped Brewer at last. 'We shall all be left to die in this filthy room full of rats.'

'That won't happen,' said Will firmly. 'Captain Drake said he would look after us all, and he will.'

They waited in the dark for a long time, listening to the thud of feet on the boards above their heads. Time passed slowly.

Suddenly the door flew open and, in the dim light, Will saw Doughty in the doorway. His heart sank and he daren't look at Brewer. Then, as he grew used to the light, Will noticed the rope around Doughty's wrists and Diego behind him.

'Make way for the traitor!' said Diego, pushing

Doughty into the room. 'Will, Captain Drake wants you on deck. I'll look after Brewer.'

Will ran up into the dazzling sunlight. Drake stood by the ship's rail, holding the drum. He came forward and handed it to Will.

'Drum up the men, Will!' he ordered. 'And keep drumming until I have their attention.'

The men gathered slowly on the deck, ashamed to look their captain in the eye. Francis Drake stared at them for a long time.

'I must have your loyalty,' he told them. 'Soon we enter the Strait of Magellan and all its dangers. We must all pull together under one command. First we must find fresh water and meat. Then Doughty will be tried before a court. This must be settled once and for all. If any man does not agree, he must speak out now, and he will also be tried for treason.'

The men moved quietly back to work. Francis Drake came over to Will.

'I have you to thank, Will Thatcher,' he said. 'My men were on the point of mutiny and poor Brewer was treated shamefully. I knew I was right to bring you along. You have served me well.'

'Land ho! Land ho!'

Will looked ahead. Port St. Julian. The last safe place to land before the dangerous Strait ahead. The stopping place of Magellan himself fifty eight years before.

'We shall all go ashore,' said Drake. 'This is where

Captain Doughty shall be tried for treason.'

It took a long time to reach the shore. It was gloomy with towering cliffs and sharp rocks where penguins huddled. The beach was bare except for a rotting gallows close to the water's edge. Frayed rope still dangled from it and Will imagined he could hear the choking cries of the men who had been hanged. The remains of skeletons poked through the sand.

Moone stood beside Will.

'Who were they?' whispered Will, shuddering.

'Magellan's mutineers,' said Moone. 'They refused to go through the Strait with him and he had them all hanged.'

It was on this bleak rock that the trial of Thomas Doughty was held. He was found guilty of mutiny and sentenced to death by Francis Drake. Doughty accepted the decision quietly and was taken back aboard the *Pelican* where he dined with his captain the night before the execution.

The next morning, to Will's surprise, Diego woke him early.

'Get up, master Will. Put on these clothes and fetch the drum. Hurry!'

'What's happening?' asked Will, looking round for Brewer and Moone; but they weren't next to him.

'Captain Doughty is to be executed,' muttered Diego and left before Will could say any more.

Will smiled with pleasure at the new clothes

Diego had left for him. His ran his hands over the smooth green velvet jacket and breeches, and the long yellow feather on the hat. He dressed quickly, fetched the drum and went on deck, ready to call the men. But they were already there, waiting and watching. Will found Brewer.

'What do you think?' he laughed, twirling round. 'Do I look as grand as the gentlemen travellers?'

'Yes,' said Brewer shortly.

'What's wrong?' asked Will.

Brewer remained silent as a tall man carrying a sword caught Will by the arm and pulled him towards the middle of the deck.

'Brewer has taught you the drum roll, I hear,' said the man.

Will nodded.

'We are ready to begin the execution,' said the man. 'When I raise my sword, start to roll the drum. When you stop, I shall bring the sword down.'

At last Will realised why he had been given the fine new clothes. He looked for Brewer in the crowd but he couldn't see him. 'Are you strong enough for the job, Will Thatcher?' Drake had asked him on Plymouth Hoe all those months ago. 'Yes,' he had replied. 'I am.' Will took a deep breath and held the drumsticks steady.

Thomas Doughty stood by the mast. Moone stepped forward to blindfold him but Doughty pushed him away and walked slowly to the middle

of the deck. He stood still, made the sign of the cross and knelt down. He stared across at Will.

Will looked away quickly to the sword which dazzled his eyes as it rose against the sun. He raised his drumsticks and rolled the drum over and over again like thunder across the sky. He had to carry on or else the terrible thing would happen! Will saw Francis Drake frown and look at him impatiently. He lifted the drumsticks high into the air and held them there. The silence was broken by the swish of the sword as it plunged down and took off Doughty's head.

Francis Drake came forward and announced

'Lo, there is the end of traitors!'

The deck tilted in the swelling sea and Will watched the head roll towards him. One of the crew ran to pick it up and held it high for the others to see. After that, Will fainted.

CHAPTER FOUR

When Will opened his eyes he remembered the terrible thing that had happened.

'I want to go home!' he whispered.

At once Brewer was at his side.

'You're all right, Will. Just lie still.'

'I'm sick of it all,' said Will. 'Nobody told me I would have to. . ..'

'You had no choice,' said Brewer. 'I should have warned you but I couldn't face it. You did your job well, that is all that matters. Now you'll need to be even braver. We'll be going into the Strait of Magellan soon. The weather is fair, thank God, but I've never seen such fear on the men's faces.'

Brewer gave Will water to drink.

'The captain will send rowing boats ahead to chart the way and they will pull us through the Strait,' he said.

'I want to go home,' said Will.

'And so you shall,' said Brewer patiently, 'but not the way you came.'

The *Pelican* sailed through the Strait of Magellan in sixteen days. Dark rocks rose up on either side and Will could almost touch them where the channel narrowed. Smoke billowed from the volcanoes but there was no fire. On the 6 September, 1578, the ships struggled out into the Pacific ocean.

Brewer did his best to cheer Will.

'What do you think now, Will? We are the first Englishmen to sail through the Strait and into the South Sea (Pacific Ocean). Now the captain can look for *Terra Australis*.'

Will didn't answer. Moone came up on deck, grumbling loudly.

'All that work,' he muttered. 'Why couldn't he make up his mind before we left Plymouth.'

'What's the matter, Moone?' asked Brewer.

'The captain's gone and given the ship a new name, that's what's the matter. And now I've got to make a new sign.'

'What's it going to be called?' asked Brewer.

'The *Golden Hind*,' said Moone. 'They say it's to thank his friend, Christopher Hatton who gave him money for this voyage. His family crest has a hind.'

'Why is it golden?' asked Will.

'You'll see soon enough!' said Moone, winking at Brewer.

Will stared out to sea.

'Captain Drake said there'd be silver monkeys,' he said. 'All I've seen so far is black rocks, and gallows and dead bodies.'

Brewer put his arm round Will's shoulders.

'It'll be plain sailing from now on, you'll see,' he said. 'We'll have to take on water soon and perhaps the captain will take you ashore with him to find your monkeys!'

Brewer had spoken too soon. Just when they thought they were out of danger, a storm sprang up and the ship was helpless in its force. They were in unknown seas and the captain was afraid they would be flung against the coast of *Terra Australis*, wherever that was. The *Golden Hind* was tossed around for more than two weeks until Will couldn't stand it any longer.

'I'm going up on deck,' said Will to Brewer.

'You can't in this storm,' said Brewer. 'It's not safe up there. Moone says we've lost sight of all the other ships except the *Marigold* and she's taking in water.'

Will picked up the drum and made for the stairs. Brewer staggered after him and found Will clutching the ship's rail and staring into the darkness.

'The *Marigold*!' yelled Will. 'I can't see her!'

'She'll be up with the next wave,' said Brewer.

They watched for the ship's lurching lanterns, but the *Marigold* had disappeared.

'She's gone!' shouted the man on watch. 'God help the poor souls for we can do nothing for them.'

'We're all going to die!' screamed Will. 'We're the only ship left! I'll save us. The drum will beat the danger away!'

Will skidded across the deck towards the ship's mast. Lashed by heavy waves, he struggled to tie himself to it with a piece of rope.

'Will! Come down!' shouted Brewer. 'It's not safe. A drum can't beat away a storm. 'You'd be better on your knees praying!'

'I can do it!' shrieked Will. 'You'll see.'

Will started to beat the drum steadily as the waves washed over him, muffling the sound. A streak of lightning struck the top of the mast and showered sparks over Will's head and into the black water below him.

'Get down!' yelled Brewer, crawling towards the mast. 'The rope won't hold you much longer!'

But Brewer kept slipping away from Will as the deck tipped.

'Leave me!' yelled Will. 'I'm safe. I've got the drum!'

Brewer left Will where he was. Will beat the drum all through the night and by dawn the wind had died down. At last the *Golden Hind* was safe. Then he let Moone and Brewer untie him and leave him to sleep on the sunlit deck.

***

He woke up to hear Francis Drake talking to Diego.

'The men are saying that your drum beat away the storm,' said Diego.

'Who knows?' said Drake. 'But there's one thing I am sure about. There is no such place as *Terra Australis*. We've been out on the ocean for a month in the worst storm I have seen in twenty years. We would have been blown on to it by now if it was there.'

'So much for the Queen's wishes, then,' said Diego. 'What now?'

'I've a mind to sail up the west coast. 'I've never been there but we have Spanish charts to guide us. Who knows what treasure ships we may find?' laughed Drake. 'There's an island marked on one of the charts, just off the coast. We'll stop there for water and fruit and perhaps do some trade with the Indians.'

Will smiled to himself. They were safe now and soon he would see silver monkeys on the island.

Will told Brewer and Moone what he had heard.

'I knew he would come back to the South Sea,' said Moone. 'I've seen that look on the captain's face before. 1573, it was, on the Spanish Main. We attacked a town to steal its treasure.'

'I was there as well, don't forget!' said Brewer. He looked at Will.

'That's where my friend was killed. I gave you his box.'

Moone broke the silence that followed.

'We could have stolen the lot,' he said, 'but the captain was shot in the leg. He nearly died from losing blood.'

'That's when Diego joined us,' said Brewer. 'He ran away from his Spanish master. I reckon he helped to save the captain's life.'

'We had to hide further up the coast after that,' said Moone. 'But not for long. The captain's not a man to run away. Especially when there's gold to be taken. He'd heard there was a mule-train leaving the port of Panama, bringing treasure from Peru. There were already Spanish ships in the Caribbean waiting to take it back to Spain.'

'So we left the ship and marched inland to find it,' said Brewer. 'We met some Indians on the way.'

'Did they attack you?' asked Will.

'No!' laughed Brewer. 'They hate the Spanish as much as we do. That's why they make good spies for us.'

'They took Drake to the top of a great tree,' said Moone. 'From behind he could see the ocean that brought him from England. But ahead there was another sea. The South Sea. Drake had never seen it before. None of us had. I tell you, he was like a man who had just seen God. Drake fell to his knees under that tree and prayed for half an hour. I knew then he'd come back one day.'

Will felt very humble. He'd been given a chance to see the wonders of a new world and all he'd done was faint and cry to go home. He would be brave from now on. After all, he was fourteen and a soft ginger beard was beginning to show on his chin.

CHAPTER FIVE

It took nearly two months to reach the island of Mocha, off the coast of Chile, as they were driven back out to sea many times by strong winds. When the ship finally put down her anchor, Will watched the men prepare to take a boat ashore.

'Ready, Sir' cried Diego. 'We must go now while the tide is high.'

'Stop fussing, man,' came Drake's voice. 'We're only taking one boat. Leave me to say my prayers.'

Will looked across at the island in amazement. He had never seen such green trees and bushes, or heard such strange noises. Were there silver monkeys out there too? He'd waited a whole year to see them and he wasn't going to be left behind.

'Wait!' he yelled down. 'Don't go without me.'

'There isn't room!' shouted Moone. 'There are ten of us already.'

'The captain promised he could come,' said Brewer, standing up in the boat. 'He can have my place.'

Francis Drake came on to the deck.

'Will, what's going on?' he said impatiently.

'Sir,' said Will.'You promised I would see silver monkeys soon.'

Drake laughed.

'So I did. Make room, men. We can squeeze him in.'

Will started to climb down the rope ladder. Suddenly he scrambled back up on deck.

'Don't leave without me,' he begged. 'I've forgotten something!'

They waited. But Drake was furious when Will came back down the ladder wearing the drum.

'In the name of God, boy, how dare you bring my drum! Take it back.'

'Please, Sir,' said Will, almost crying. 'I've got to take it. I don't know why, but I've got to.'

Drake stared at Will's worried face and remembered how he had drummed away the mutiny and the great storm. His face softened.

'Very well,' he said 'but I shall deal with you later, Will Thatcher. And if there's a mark on my drum, you shall pay dearly for it.'

They reached the island. The sun beat down fiercely and they made for the shade of the trees. Bright birds flew among the long yellow fruits hanging from the branches. Will walked ahead with Brewer, eager to see the monkeys. He heard a rustling sound. Will stared at the bushes, sweat trickling down his back. Two dark eyes stared back at him then there was a silver flash.

'It's a silver monkey!' shouted Will, and he ran forward, followed closely by Brewer.

As he ran, a silver tip spun through the air, past Will's ear and thudded into the ground behind him. Will turned to see an arrow quivering in the sand.

'Get down!' he said to Brewer. Will raised his hands into the air and beat the drum with his fists.

The others ran back towards the rowing boat as soon as they heard the drum. But it was too late for Diego. An arrow pierced his back and he died where he fell. Will grabbed hold of Brewer and they ran to join the others. More arrows flew from the bushes. Will let go of Brewer's arm and held the drum above their heads as they ran. A cloud of arrows rushed past them, some piercing the drum skin. Soon they were away from the bushes and nearing the safety of the boat.

'We must fire, Sir,' shouted Moone.

'No,' said Drake sadly. 'Diego would not have wanted me to. They only attacked us because they thought we were Spanish men come to rob them. We will prove we are above such things. The drum will protect them.'

Will and Brewer staggered through the water to the boat. The men dragged them aboard and rowed quickly back to the *Golden Hind*. Will sat holding the drum tightly to him, trying hard not to cry. It had

saved them all except for Diego. There was a splash of bright red on the yellow globe. He touched it and his fingers were stained with blood. He looked up at Drake beside him.

'Sir,' said Will. 'You are wounded.'

Drake wiped his cheek.

'The arrow grazed me as I ran. Thank God it was not poisonous, or else I should be dead in the sand with Diego, God rest his soul.'

'I'm sorry about your drum,' said Will.

'I'm not,' said Drake, 'for it saved our lives. Moone can mend it easily enough.'

They reached the ship, pulled up anchor and sailed straight away. Drake spent days alone in his cabin, deeply upset by the death of Diego who had been with him for so many years. Will took the drum to Moone for repair and stayed with Brewer to watch.

'Poor old drum,' said Will.

'I'd rather the holes were in it than in our heads,' said Brewer, shuddering as he remembered the silver tipped arrows.

'I only wanted to see a silver monkey,' said Will. 'Do you think the captain will go straight back to England now?'

Moone laughed as he stretched a new skin over the drum.

'And miss all the fun! That's the best bit, robbing

the Spanish and frightening them half to death! Don't forget, young Will, this is the first time Drake has been on this coast. You wait, this ship will soon earn the name of *Golden*.'

'But that's stealing!' cried Will.

'They deserve it,' said Brewer. 'Years ago, when Captain Drake first went to sea, to take African slaves to the Spanish Main, he was attacked by the Spanish for no reason. Only fifteen men out of four hundred made it back to England! These Spanish dogs deserve all they get. They are plundering this land and they will do the same to England if they get the chance. Philip is a cruel king and we are right to hate him.'

'How will we get home?' asked Will.

'I think the captain will go up the coast and look for a way back round the top of America,' said Moone. 'That's further than any ship has ever been.'

Moone was right. They sailed past Panama, capturing so much treasure that the *Golden Hind* was full. Further north, beyond California, the weather grew cold and ice hung thickly on the rigging. It was only when the ship began to leak that Drake gave the order to turn south again.

'Are we going back to England through the Strait again?' Will asked Brewer.

'I don't know,' said Brewer. 'Have you heard anything, Moone?'

'I have,' said Moone. 'We're sailing west through the South Sea to the Philippine Islands.'

'Good God!' shouted Brewer, leaping up and hitting his head on the timbers above. 'Do you know what that means? God willing, if we reach England safely from here, we shall be the first Englishmen to sail round the world, just like Magellan's ships.'

'And we all know what happened to Magellan,' said Moone.

'Will doesn't,' said Brewer. 'Tell him, Moone.'

Moone put his face close to Will's and whispered

'Killed by the Indians before he got back to Portugal.'

It was a long time before Will fell asleep.

***

For two months the *Golden Hind* sailed through an empty sunlit sea until they came to the Philippine Islands.

Will and Brewer were in the first boat to go ashore. Will ran along the beach looking up at the trees as a flash of light caught his eye.

'I should have brought the drum!' said Will. 'What if there are Indians hiding in the trees? What if they shoot arrows at us!'

'These are friendly islands,' said Brewer. 'They are used to visitors. Let's hope the monkeys are as friendly.'

'I heard a squeal, up there!' yelled Will.

He looked more closely. A long silver shape clung to the branches. It swung round to reveal a small face with huge black eyes. Will jumped up and down in the sand, shouting and waving to the others.

'I think young Will has just seen a silver monkey,' laughed Drake. 'Two years is a long time to wait!'

The monkey ran to the top of the tree and threw down hard brown fruits. One split open as it hit the ground and milk spilled into the sand.

'It's a coco nut,' said Brewer. 'Like the one the captain uses at table, set inside a silver goblet. Diego once showed it to me.'

'Poor Diego,' said Will. 'I wish he was with us now.'

They took fresh water and fruit to the ship. Drake paced up and down, impatient to sail.

'I'm weary of this long voyage,' he said. 'Can you believe a new year has begun? 1580! I want to go home.'

They pulled up anchor and set off into strong winds. Francis Drake was tense and jumpy because the waters were largely unmapped. Just one mistake and his ship could be the lost. A gloom settled over them all.

'It's worse than the Strait of Magellan,' said Brewer, 'I don't like it. Keep the drum by you, Will, there's terrible danger out there.

***

It happened just past midnight. In a strong wind, the *Golden Hind* struck an island reef. The water behind was too deep for them to lay anchor to pull her off. The wind grew worse and pushed them further on to the reef. They were stranded high out of the water, lashed by huge waves which washed across the lower deck.

'It's our punishment for putting Doughty to death!' wailed Will.

'None of that talk, Will Thatcher!' bellowed Drake. 'Now set to. We must try to free the ship.'

They worked all night under the swaying lanterns but the ship remained where she was. The morning light revealed how dangerous their situation was but all work stopped for prayers.

'Be of good heart,' said the Francis Drake to his frightened men. 'Now we have looked after your souls, you had better look after your bodies as best you can. I fear the worst. We are in greater danger than we have been since leaving England. We must lighten the ship's load.'

He called Will over to him.

'Beat the drum, Will, if only to give us courage!'

Throughout the day, six guns were thrown overboard, and barrels of beer and spices.

'But leave the treasure where it is!' ordered Drake.

Suddenly the ship lurched into the air and came to rest higher on the reef.

'Prepare to save yourselves,' ordered Drake to the men praying on the deck. 'Each man for himself.'

At that moment, the wind changed direction. The *Golden Hind* was blown into the deep water behind her and began to float free of the reef. The men cheered and Will waved the drum in the air, staggering as the ship rolled violently, suddenly free of the reef.

Will grabbed at the ship's rail but it was too late.

'Help!' he shrieked. 'I'm falling!'

'Man overboard!' someone shouted. 'Throw down a rope!'

Will thought he would never reach the water. He closed his eyes and clutched the drum as the wind took his breath away. At last, he hit the waves and sank beneath them. Terrified, Will opened his eyes and saw the sun shining through the water. He couldn't breathe but just when he thought his lungs would burst, Will was catapulted upwards and he shot above the water, like a ball from a cannon.

'Hold on!' shouted Brewer. 'We're letting down the boat.'

Will, panic-stricken, held his breath and waited to go under the water again. Suddenly, he realised he was floating.

'I'm safe,' he shouted. 'The drum's holding me up.'

Ten minutes later, Will was hauled out of the water and lay shivering at the bottom of the boat.

'I've spoiled the captain's drum,' he muttered, his teeth chattering.

'Least of your worries,' said Moone. 'It'll soon dry out. Be thankful it saved your life, lad. And not for the first time.'

'Prepare the sails!' shouted Drake.

'Where to, captain?' came the reply.

Drake's voice sounded loud and clear. 'England.'

CHAPTER SIX

Will and Brewer lay wide awake on deck, shivering in the chilly September air. They were in sight of England now and tomorrow the *Golden Hind* would sail into Plymouth.

'They'll never believe me at home when I tell them I've been Drake's drummer boy and sailed right round the world,' said Will.

'I've no one to tell,' said Brewer. 'I've been on my own since I was twelve. That's why I went to sea.'

'Where will you go?' asked Will.

'Don't worry about me,' said Brewer. 'The captain will keep a few of us on. He has to in case the Queen sends for him and we have to sail to the Thames.'

'Do you think we'll ever sail together again?' asked Will.

'Yes,' said Brewer firmly. 'You'll see.'

The *Golden Hind* anchored at dawn at a small island a mile from Plymouth harbour. Will paced up and down the deck wearing the drum. Drake caught sight of him and his face turned red with anger.

'Take off my drum, boy,' he snapped. 'Put it back in the oak chest. It's work is done. Make sure you wrap it carefully.'

'But, Sir. . ..began Will, 'we're back in Plymouth.'

'And I can never be sure of the welcome I receive,' said Drake. 'That is why we have not gone into harbour yet. Last time, the Queen made me go away and hide. Can you believe it? I am the first Englishman to sail his own ship right round the world and when I return, with six hundred thousand pounds, I have to wait to be told what I may do. Remember Will, we are her Majesty's servants. Never forget that.'

The *Golden Hind* lay at anchor off Plymouth for several days. Will sat on the deck, drumming his fingers with impatience, staring at the tall houses in the distance. It was not the homecoming he had expected.

Suddenly he caught the smell of lavender and roses. He turned and saw a woman wearing a white gown embroidered with gold, and over it, a fur-lined velvet cloak. A silk net held back her hair and ropes of pearls covered her long neck. Will looked down at his filthy clothes, at the bites and sores on his skin and he felt ashamed.

He leapt to his feet and gave a short bow.

'Welcome aboard, your Majesty,' he said, wishing he had his drum to beat.

To his surprise, the lady threw back her head and

laughed. This sound brought Francis Drake up on deck and he kissed the woman, and spun her round.

'Will,' he called out. 'This is my wife, Mary, the most beautiful woman in England!'

Will blushed and bowed again

'My dear,' said Drake, 'is the Queen alive and well?'

'Her Majesty is in good health, Sir.'

'I have sent word to her of my return,' said Drake.

'Remember how difficult it is for the Queen,' said his wife gently. 'They say the King of Spain is going to invade Portugal. And he has asked our Queen to return all his stolen treasure. If she doesn't, he might invade England as well.'

'So her Majesty will have me hide yet again,' said Drake bitterly. 'But she will want the fortune I bring back. She will say she knows nothing of it, like last time.'

'Sail into the harbour,' said his wife. 'You have nothing to fear from the Queen.'

The *Golden Hind* slipped into the harbour at dusk. Will knew it was time to leave the drum and Brewer behind. When Francis Drake was dining with the Mayor of Plymouth, he let himself into the captain's empty cabin. Will opened the oak chest and took out the drum. He said the strange words out aloud. *Sic magna parvis.* 'Big things from small beginnings.' He put the drum back in the chest and quickly left the cabin.

Will fetched his wooden box and went to find Brewer. Already the deck was crowded with men waiting to take boats back to shore. Brewer was watching from the prow.

'I'll be going ashore soon,' said Will. 'I've brought back your friend's box.'

Brewer smiled at him.

'Keep it, Will,' he said. 'It's yours now.'

'Thank you,' said Will.

'Will? Will Thatcher?' The voice came from across the water.

Will looked down.

'Father!' he shouted back. 'Are you all well?'

'Yes,' his father shouted back. 'And thank God you're safe, Will. We thought we'd never see you again. We didn't know you'd be away so long. You have a new brother, Edward. Born this last week. I've come to take you home.'

Will turned to Brewer.

'Goodbye,' he said simply.

Brewer tugged Will's beard.

'They won't recognise you at home!' he laughed.

'And is my drummer boy leaving without saying goodbye?'

Will blushed as red as his beard as Francis Drake came up and shook him by the hand.

'Goodbye, Sir,' said Will.

'Goodbye, Will Thatcher,' said Drake. 'There will be trouble before long with the King of Spain. Then I shall need you and my drum. Will you sail with us again, drummer boy?'

Will smiled at Brewer, then turned to Francis Drake.

'Yes, Sir,' said Will. 'I'll come with you.'

And he did. But that's another story.

Sixteen years later . . . .

'My drum? Where's my drum?' muttered Sir Francis Drake, trying to sit up.

'Lie still,' said his chaplain. 'You've got the fever. You must rest, we're safe now. Let us take off your armour.'

'Leave it. I shall die like a soldier,' whispered Drake. 'It's my fault. All my fault. I shouldn't have stopped on the way here. It gave our Spanish enemies time to lie in wait for us. When the fever's gone, we'll go back to the shore. I came to capture Panama, and, by God, I will.'

The chaplain sighed as he looked around him. Men lay all over the deck of the *Defiance*, groaning and shivering and too weak to move.

Suddenly, Drake shouted

'Will Thatcher! Bring me my drum!'

A tall ginger-haired boy stepped forward and held up a drum. The sun glinted on its coat of arms and showed up worn patches on the leather strap. Sir Francis Drake put out his hand and touched it, smiling and quiet now.

'This drum has saved us from many a beating, hasn't it, Will?'

'My name is Edward, Sir. Edward Thatcher. Will is my older brother.'

'So he is,' said Drake. 'He was a fine drummer boy too. Sailed right round the world with me. And drummed the Spanish Armada back up the

Channel. Come closer, Edward.'

The boy crouched down to catch the captain's words.

'Take my drum back to England. If ever England is in danger, I shall come back from heaven and beat it. Have it put in my home at Buckland Abbey. Promise.'

'I promise, Sir Francis,' whispered Edward.

Sir Francis Drake died a few hours later. The next day, January 27, 1596, as Drake's coffin slipped into the warm waters of the Caribbean sea, Edward Thatcher rolled the drum just as his brother Will had taught him.

AUTHOR'S NOTE

When Francis Drake sailed from Plymouth in 1577, Elizabeth I had been on the English throne since 1558. She had chosen to make England a Protestant country (like her father Henry VIII). Philip II, the King of Spain, was angry as he hoped that England would be a Catholic country, like Spain.

The ill-feeling over religion was increased by events in the Spanish Main. This was the name given to Peru, Mexico and the Caribbean where thousands of Spanish settlers went to mine for gold. English seamen raided Spanish ships, ports and mule trains handling this treasure. Francis Drake was one of them. He wanted revenge on the Spanish who attacked him years before when he was delivering a cargo of slaves.

This put Elizabeth I in a difficult position. She liked Francis Drake and needed the gold he brought her. However, in public, she often rejected him in order to keep the peace with Spain.

By 1585, however, England was at war with Spain and three years later, Philip II sent the Armada to invade England. Sir Francis Drake (he had been knighted on his return from his voyage around the world) helped in its defeat.

In Francis Drake's day, the Strait of Magellan was believed to divide the American continent from a huge southern continent called Terra Australis. In the fierce storm after leaving the Strait, Drake's ship was blown south against an island. This is believed to be Horn Island, and it is now thought that Francis

Drake may have discovered Cape Horn itself.

I have called the places visited by Francis Drake by the names that are used today.

Drake's Drum can be seen in the Drake Gallery at Buckland Abbey. Although it was used on Drake's voyages, there is no evidence that this particular drum was taken on the voyage around the world. The legend of Drake's Drum dates back to Drake's last voyage. As he was dying, he ordered the drum to be sent back to England. He vowed that if ever England was in danger, his drum would beat by itself to summon Drake back from heaven to defend his country. The drum was heard beating during both world wars.

Francis Drake's nephew, John, and Drake's brother, Thomas, sailed with him around the world but they have not been included in this story. There is no recorded name of any drummer boy. Moone, the carpenter, and Brewer, the trumpeter, were real characters.

PLACES TO VISIT

Audley End House, Saffron Walden, Essex

Buckland Abbey, Near Plymouth, Devon
(The Drake Gallery contains Drake's Drum)

Devonport, Plymouth, Devon
(HMS Drake displays Drake's goblet and Drake's sword)

Elizabethan House Museum,
Great Yarmouth, Norfolk

Hampton Court Palace, London

Hardwick Hall, Derbyshire

Hatfield House, Hatfield, Hertfordshire

Ingatestone Hall, Chelmsford, Essex

Kentwell Hall, Long Melford, Suffolk
(Tudor re-creations each summer)

Oxburgh Hall, Norfolk